William's Dinosaurs

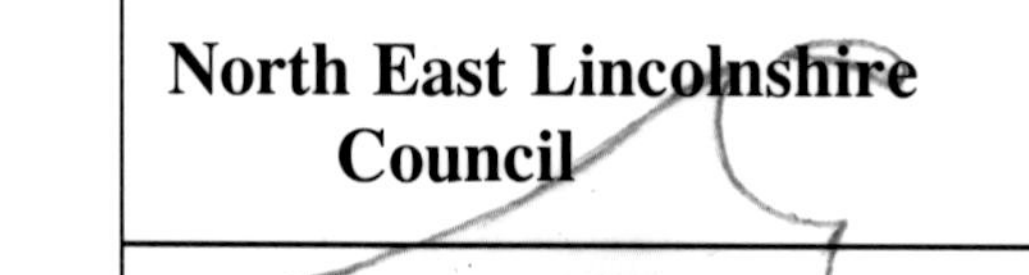

The last thing

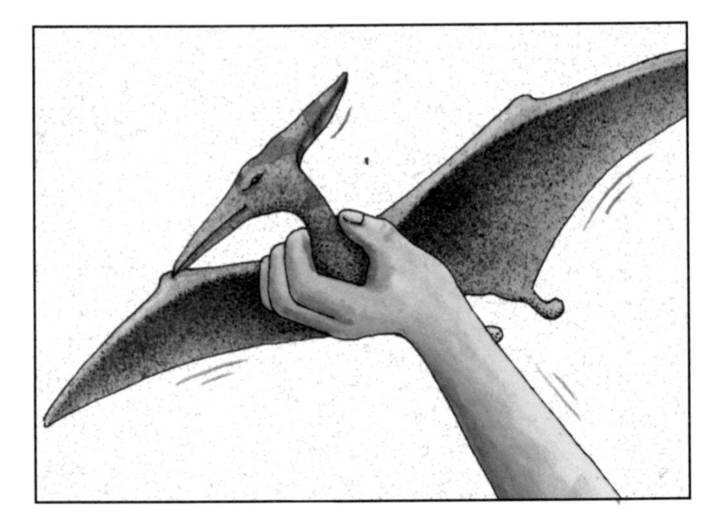

that William expected

as he played
with his
dinosaurs...

… was to feel hot and sleepy.

So he wandered into the woods
at the end of his garden.

But down
in the woods,
there was
nothing but
trees...

...and nothing
to do.

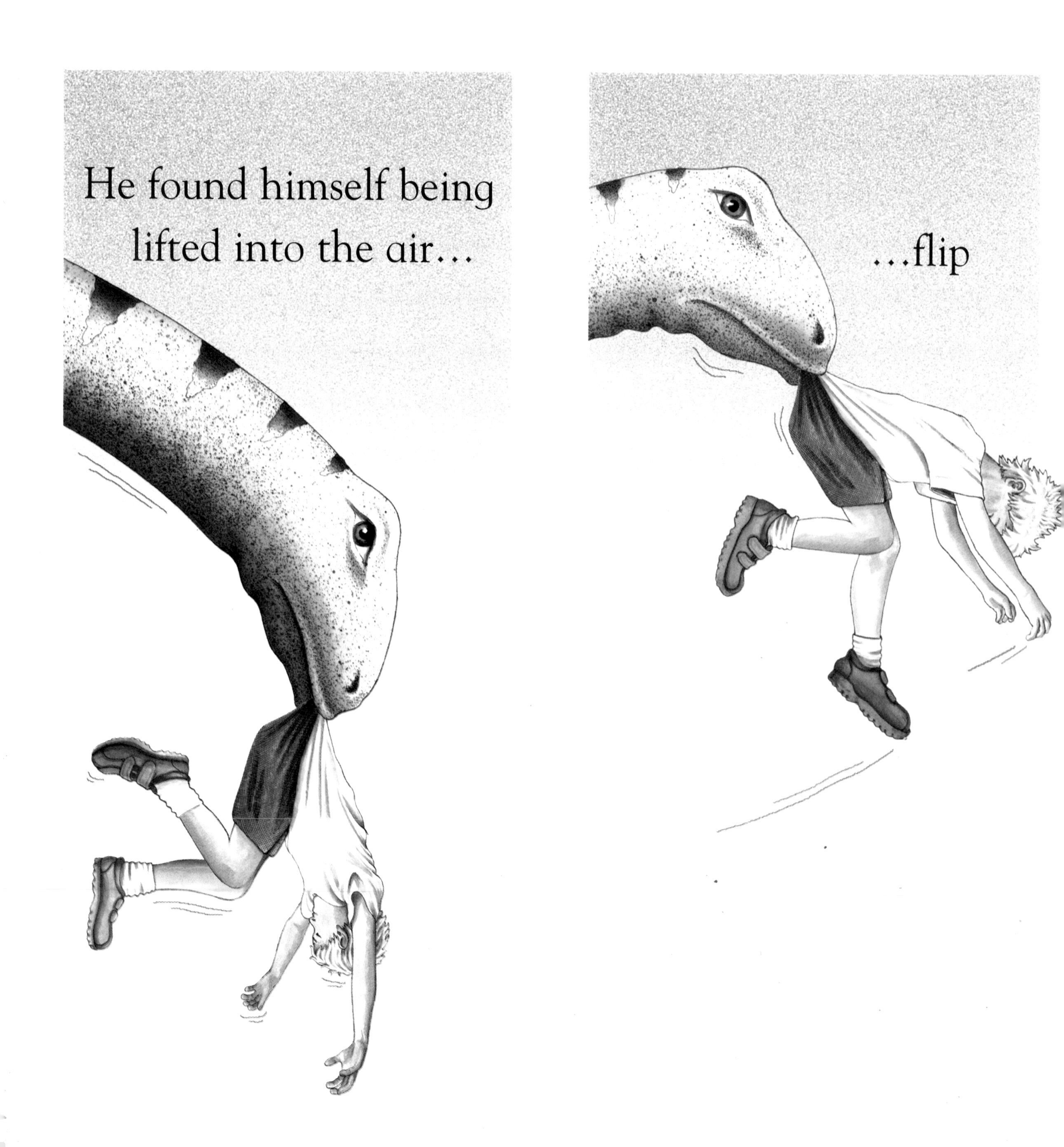
He found himself being lifted into the air…
…flip

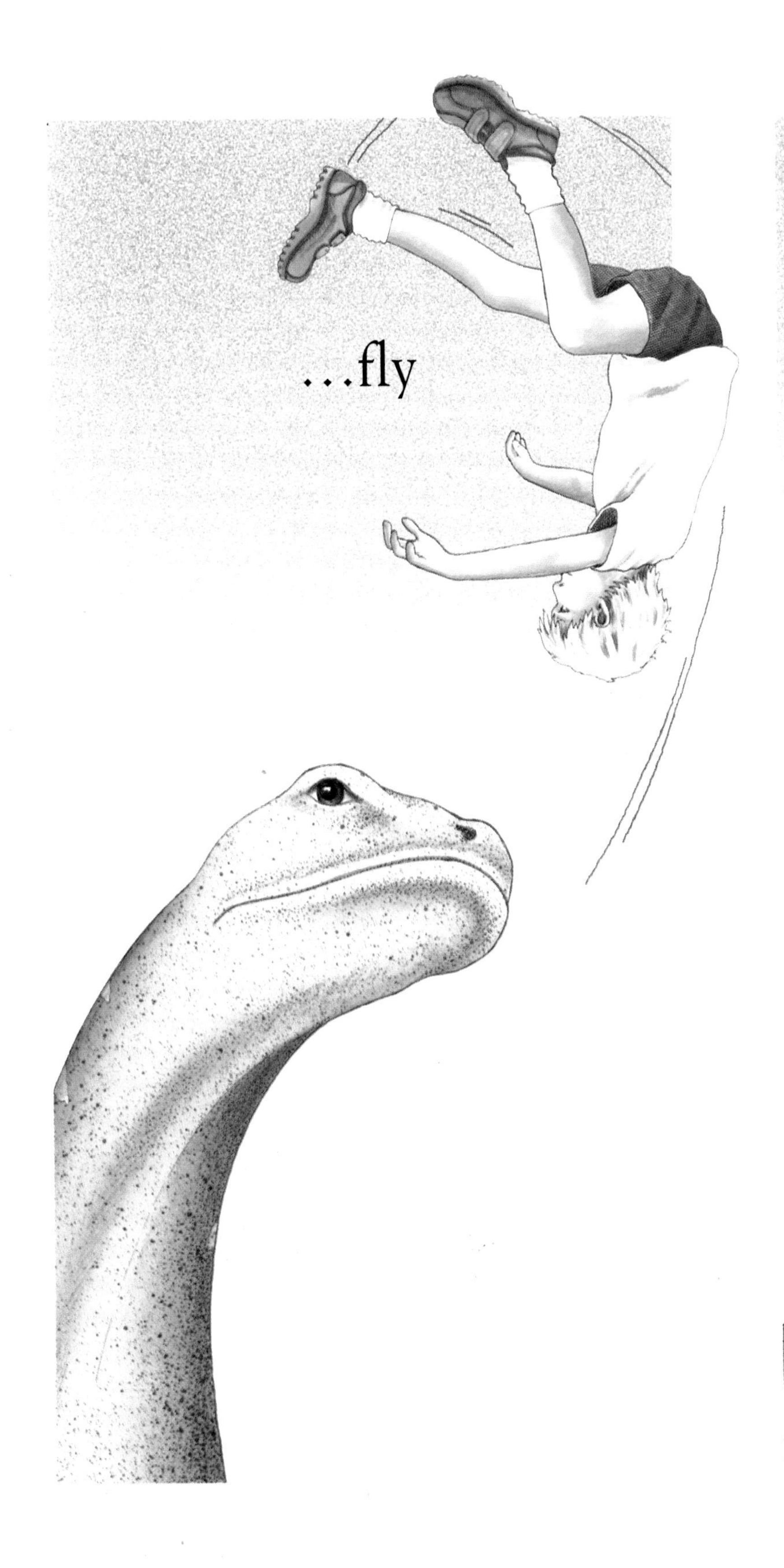

…fly

…flick, and he landed on the head of a big Brontosaurus.

He slid down the neck, down the body,

to the tail,

flick…

...and he flew through the tree-tops, landing softly in the highest of branches,

where the leaves rustled
and through the branches
sniffed and snuffled
a Tyrannosaurus.

William jumped
and
fell
from
the
branch...

...on to the back
of a drifting
Pterodactyl...

…which soared, swooped
and dived through the skies.

William could
see for miles…

...so he jumped
and fell...

...down

…down

…and into the lake

…where a passing Plesiosaur gently blew him to the sandy shore.

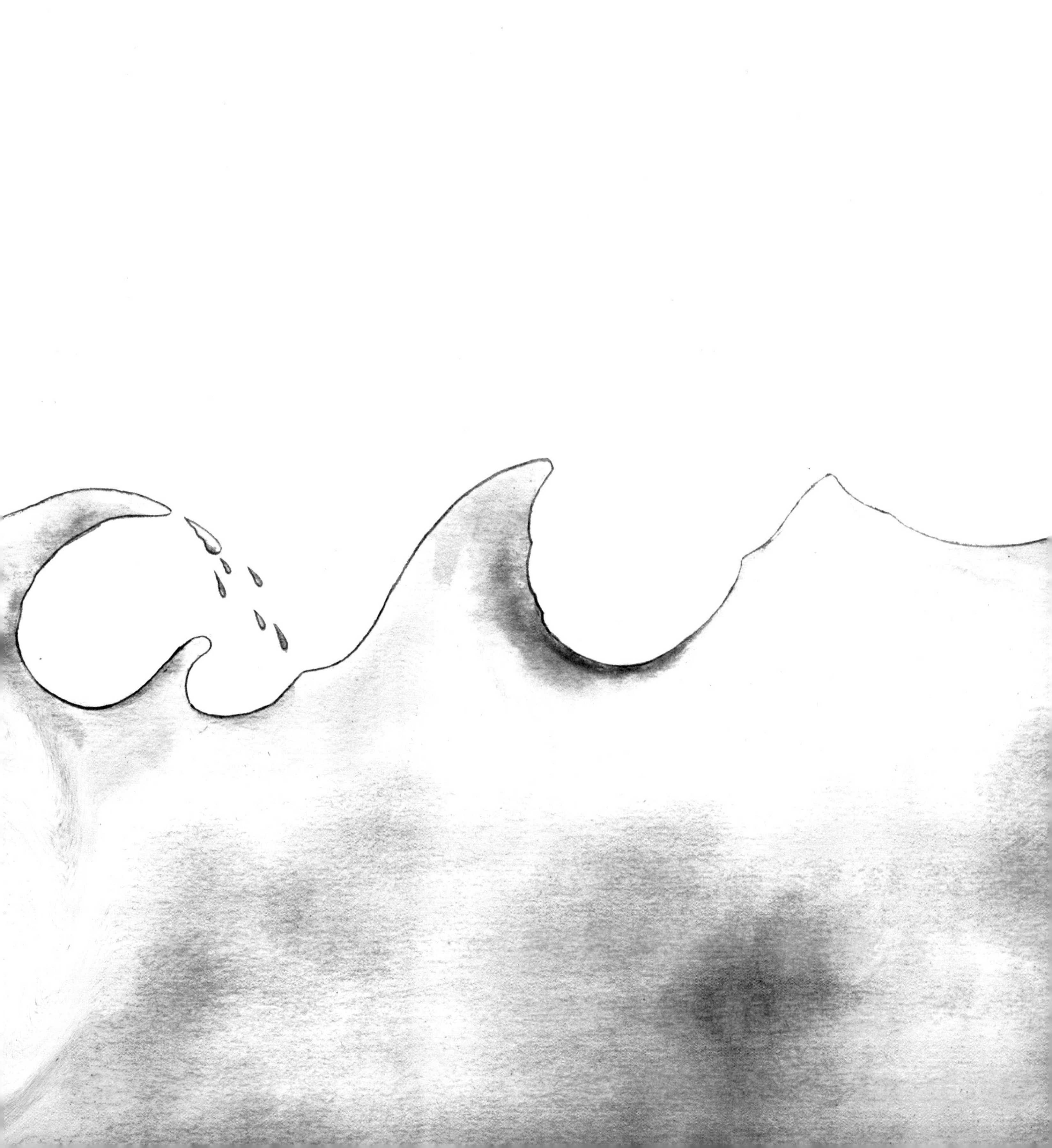

"I wonder if I fell asleep," thought William.

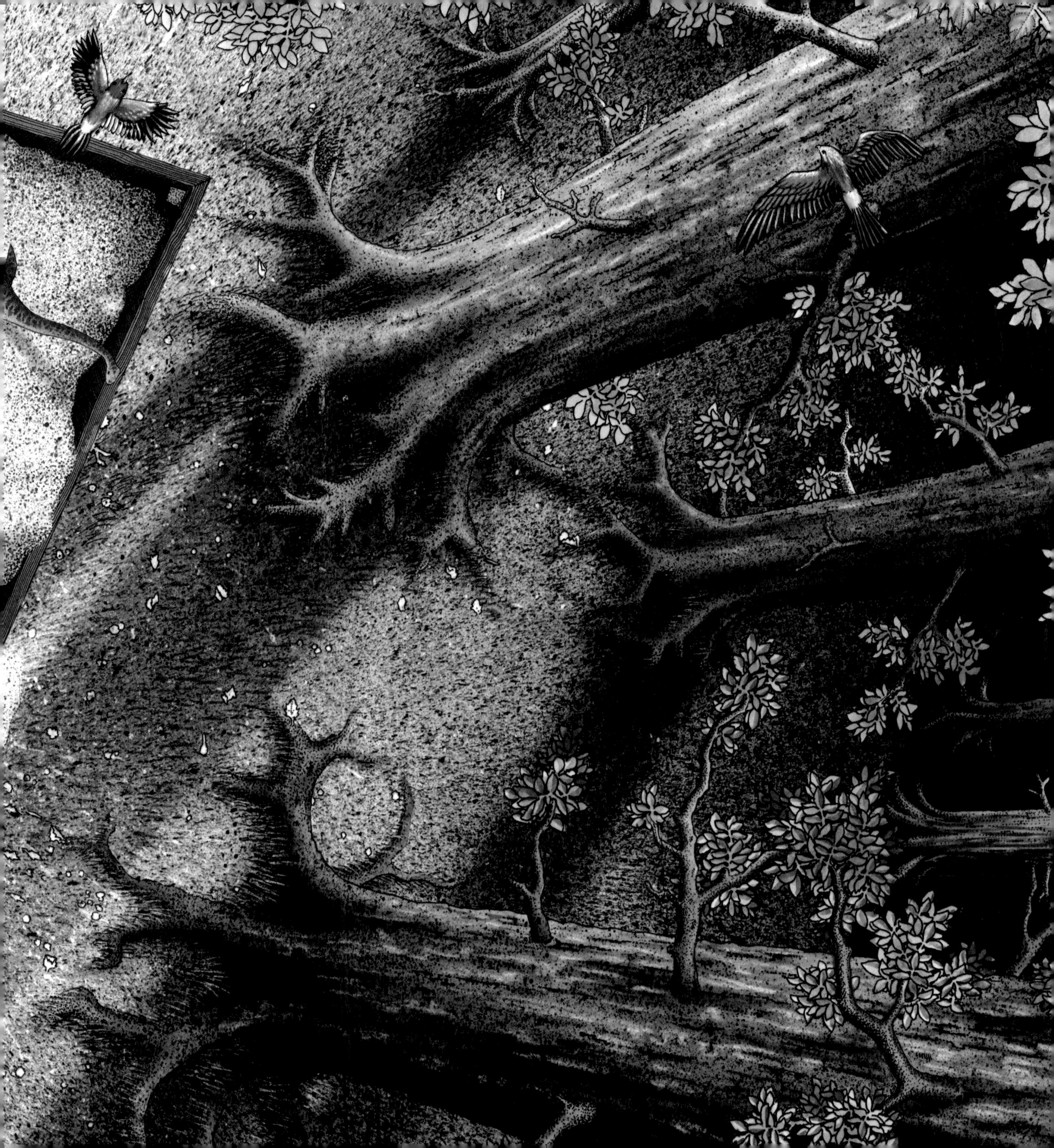

To William,

Thanks for your help.

A.B.

First published in 2005 by Meadowside Children's Books,
185 Fleet Street, London, EC4A 2HS

A CIP catalogue record for this book is available from the British Library
Printed in U.A.E

10 9 8 7 6 5 4 3 2 1